KT-417-982

CONTENTS

THE AMAZING ADVENTURES OF THE DC SUPER-PETS!

Horse Show Heist

by **Steve Korté**

illustrated by **Art Baltazar**

Supergirl based on characters created by Jerry Siegel and Joe Shuster by special arrangement with the Jerry Siegel Family

Raintree is an imprint of Capstone Global Library Limited, a company incorporated in England and Wales having its registered office at 264 Banbury Road, Oxford, OX2 7DY – Registered company number: 6695582

www.raintree.co.uk
myorders@raintree.co.uk

ISBN 978 1 3982 1498 9

Designed by Ted Williams
Design Elements by Shutterstock/SilverCircle
Printed and bound in India

British Library Cataloguing in Publication Data
A full catalogue record for this book is available from the British Library.

He can fly through the
air and read minds.
He shares the same powers
as Supergirl, his loyal friend.

These are . . .

THE AMAZING
ADVENTURES OF
Comet the
Super-horse!

CHAPTER 1

Interesting pets

Kara Danvers is relaxing in her

college room. Kara is Supergirl's secret

identity.

Kara is playing with her Super-Cat, Streaky. She throws a ball of wool into the air. Streaky flies after it.

The wool gets tangled in a whirling ceiling fan!

Streaky uses his super-strength to pull

on the wool, but he accidentally pulls

the fan out of the ceiling.

The fan crashes to the ground!

"Streaky, you have to be more careful about using your superpowers!" scolds Kara. "I don't want anyone to find out that I'm Supergirl!"

Just then, Kara hears Comet the Super-horse whinny. She looks round just in time to see Comet flying next to her second-storey window!

"Comet, what if someone sees you?" Kara asks. She is worried. "I am going to take you to a stable. You can pretend that you are an ordinary horse."

CHAPTER 2

Comet, the ordinary horse

The next day, Kara meets the owner of the stable.

The owner is surprised to see that Comet is not wearing any horseshoes.

"We can take care of that for you,"

says the owner.

Oh, no! thinks Kara.

She knows it's impossible to nail

horseshoes to Comet's super-hard

hooves. The owner will know straight

away that Comet is not a normal horse.

But Kara has an idea. She offers to do

the job herself. When no one is looking,

she uses her heat vision. It melts the

metal shoes to Comet's hooves.

That afternoon, Kara takes Comet for

a ride. Comet leaps high over a fence.

"Wow, that's great jumping!" says the owner of the stable. "We're having a horse show tomorrow. It's going to raise a lot of money for charity."

Kara smiles at Comet. She fills in an entry form.

CHAPTER 3

Super save

The next day, Kara and Comet are

trotting around the ring with other

horses and riders.

Suddenly, a large grey lorry zooms past them. Comet turns his head and looks at the lorry.

Comet uses his mind-reading powers on the lorry's passengers. He learns that they have just stolen the charity money from the stable!

Comet leaps over the fence and

gallops after the lorry.

"What is it, Comet?" asks Kara. "Is there something bad in that lorry?"

Kara tries to use her X-ray vision. It doesn't work! The lorry must be covered in lead. That is the one metal that Kara can't see through.

Kara looks around. They're all alone.

She changes into her Supergirl outfit.

"Okay, Comet," she says. "No one

can see us. Let's go!"

Comet lands in front of the lorry. The vehicle screeches to a halt when the driver sees a horse in the road

Comet turns around. He kicks the lorry with his powerful legs.

Comet then kicks a hole in the
lorry's side. Two men jump out.
They are carrying bags of cash.

Supergirl grabs the two men by the back of their shirts. She flies them to the police station.

Supergirl and Comet return the stolen money. She gives Comet a big hug. He gets a carrot for a job well done.

"Here's to a speedy, quick-thinking Super-horse who has his own secret identity," she says. "Those men will think twice before they decide to steal again."

Comet nuzzles Supergirl and chomps his carrot.

AUTHOR!

Steve Korté is the author of many books for children and young adults. He worked at DC Comics for many years, editing more than 600 books about Superman, Batman, Wonder Woman and the other heroes and villains in the DC Universe. He lives in New York City, USA, with his husband, Bill, and their super-cat, Duke.

ILLUSTRATOR!

Famous cartoonist Art Baltazar is the creative force behind *The New York Times* bestselling, Eisner Award-winning DC Comics' Tiny Titans; co-writer for Billy Batson and the Magic of Shazam, Young Justice, Green Lantern Animated (Comic); and artist/co-writer for the awesome Tiny Titans/Little Archie crossover, Superman Family Adventures, Super Powers, and Itty Bitty Hellboy! Art is one of the founders of Aw Yeah Comics comic shop and the ongoing comic series. Aw yeah, living the dream! He stays at home and draws comics and never has to leave the house! He lives with his lovely wife, Rose, sons Sonny and Gordon, and daughter, Audrey! AW YEAH MAN! Visit him at www.artbaltazar.com

"Word Power"

charity a group that raises money or collects goods to help people in need

horseshoe a U-shaped metal plate nailed to a horse's hoof in order to protect it

lead a grey metal that is softer than many other metals

nuzzle to push up or rub against gently

stable a building in which animals are kept, fed and cared for

trot to move at a speed faster than a walk

X-ray vision the ability to see inside a person or through objects

WRITING PROMPTS

1. What if the story was told by another competitor at the horse show? Write what you think they saw.

2. Write a story as though you were the handyman who had to repair Kara's ceiling fan. What would you think if you saw it?

3. Draw a poster advertising the horse show.

DISCUSSION QUESTIONS

1. Why do you think it was important that Comet and Streaky didn't show their superpowers?

2. Have you ever seen someone doing something they shouldn't have been doing? What did you do?

3. What other mischief do you think Comet and Streaky could get into? Imagine other adventures that are funny or strange.